An earwig? Eww, gross!

"What are you doing?" Mary asked.

"Digging," Harry replied.

The tunnel he was digging had reached the other side of the fence into the vacant lot.

"You shouldn't do that, Harry," Mary scolded.

Suddenly Sid appeared.

Harry held up an earwig by its pincers. I didn't know which was more gross. The bug or Harry's dirty fingernails.

"Aaaaaauuuuugh!" Sidney screamed, then he took off like a roadrunner!

I just cringed.

Harry really does love horrible things.

OTHER BOOKS IN THE
HORRIBLE HARRY SERIES

Horrible Harry
Bugs the Three Bears

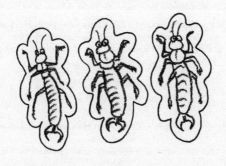

BY SUZY KLINE

Pictures by Frank Remkiewicz

PUFFIN BOOKS

PUFFIN BOOKS
Published by the Penguin Group
Penguin Young Readers Group, 345 Hudson Street, New York, New York 10014, U.S.A.
Penguin Group (Canada), 90 Eglinton Avenue East, Suite 700,
Toronto, Ontario, Canada M4P 2Y3 (a division of Pearson Penguin Canada Inc.)
Penguin Books Ltd, 80 Strand, London WC2R 0RL, England
Penguin Ireland, 25 St Stephen's Green, Dublin 2, Ireland (a division of Penguin Books Ltd)
Penguin Group (Australia), 250 Camberwell Road, Camberwell, Victoria 3124, Australia
(a division of Pearson Australia Group Pty Ltd)
Penguin Books India Pvt Ltd, 11 Community Centre,
Panchsheel Park, New Delhi - 110 017, India
Penguin Group (NZ), 67 Apollo Drive, Rosedale, North Shore 0632, New Zealand
(a division of Pearson New Zealand Ltd)
Penguin Books (South Africa) (Pty) Ltd, 24 Sturdee Avenue,
Rosebank, Johannesburg 2196, South Africa

Registered Offices: Penguin Books Ltd, 80 Strand, London WC2R 0RL, England

First published in the United States of America by Viking,
a division of Penguin Young Readers Group, 2008
Published by Puffin Books, a division of Penguin Young Readers Group, 2009

9 10

Text copyright © Suzy Kline, 2008
Illustrations copyright © Frank Remkiewicz, 2008
All rights reserved

THE LIBRARY OF CONGRESS HAS CATALOGED THE VIKING EDITION AS FOLLOWS:
Kline, Suzy.
Horrible Harry bugs the three bears / by Suzy Kline ; pictures by Frank Remkiewicz.
p. cm.
Summary: Harry incorporates his fascination with earwigs into Miss Mackle's class
project of acting out a fairy tale in front of the other third graders.
ISBN: 978-0-670-06293-5 (hc)
[1. Earwigs—Fiction. 2. Fairy tales—Fiction. 3. Theater—Fiction.
4. Schools—Fiction.] I. Remkiewicz, Frank, ill. II. Title.
Pz7.K6797Hntb 2008.
[Fic]—dc22
2007023120

Puffin Books ISBN 978-0-14-241295-4

Printed in the United States of America

Set in New Century Schoolbook

Dedicated with love
and bear hugs
to my five precious grandchildren:
Jacob, Mikenna, Gabrielle, Saylor, and Holden.
I am so thankful for each one of you!

Special appreciation to . . .

Ethan D. Fitz, who is an expert in earwigs, at Hilliard Elementary School in Westlake, Ohio. Thank you for sharing your report with me on "Extraordinary Earwigs." Your picture in the maple tree inspired this story.

Sara Jo Sites at Glenwood School in Vestal, New York, and her school's Starlight Café and Rights of the Round Table.

My granddaughter Mikenna Rose Hurtuk, who read the first manuscript and kept it on her bed.

My husband, Rufus, for his insight and titles.

Frank Remkiewicz, who understands the characters so well.

And my wonderful editor, Catherine Frank. Thank you for your valuable help with this story.

Contents

Horrible Harry
Bugs the Three Bears

Digging for Edward

My name is Doug. I'm in third grade. Harry and I have been best friends since kindergarten.

I know he loves horrible things.

I didn't know he could find them everywhere!

Each day this week at recess, I asked him, "Want to play kickball?"

And each day Harry gave me the same answer: "Not now, Doug. I'm busy."

This morning, Mary even noticed. I

was leaning on the playground fence while Harry was down on his knees.

"How come you guys aren't playing kickball like usual? What are you doing?" she asked.

"Digging," Harry replied.

I just shrugged as I looked down at Harry. The tunnel he was digging had

reached the other side of the fence into the vacant lot.

"You shouldn't do that, Harry," Mary scolded. "You're getting dirt all over yourself! You might track it into our classroom. Remember the time we got muddy footprints on our moon rug? We got in big trouble!" Then she skipped back to the jump-rope game. It was Ida's turn, and the girls were chanting:

"Ida, Ida,
Riding through the glen.
Ida, Ida,
With her band of men.
Feared by the frogs,
Loved by the dogs,
Ida, Ida.
Ida, Ida.
Ida, Ida."

The girls were having more fun than I was!

Suddenly Sid appeared. He had a green fairy-tale book tucked under his arm. "Hey, you guys want to hear something interesting? The numbers three and seven are in a lot of fairy tales!"

"No kidding?" Harry replied. "Want to see something interesting, Sid?"

Harry held up an earwig by its pincers. I didn't know which was more gross. The bug or Harry's dirty fingernails.

"*Aaaaauuuugh!*" Sidney screamed, then he took off like a roadrunner!

I just cringed.

Harry shook his head as he put the bug gently in a tissue. "Edward was dead as a doornail when I found him," he said.

"Edward?" I repeated.

"The poor guy should have a name," Harry said sadly. "He must have died last night. He still looks good, though. I'll make sure he gets buried in a garden."

I watched Harry bring the corners of the tissue together and tuck Edward gently into his pocket.

And then he started digging again!

Harry really does love horrible things.

Sometimes he spends more time with them than me!

I shuffled over to the kickball game and played left field. When I dropped the fly ball, I missed Harry calling out, "You'll catch the next one, Doug!"

That Thursday morning things got worse. Room 3B was in the library. Our teacher, Miss Mackle, was reminding us of our homework.

"Remember, boys and girls," she said. "The third-grade classes are studying fairy tales. Pick one that your literature circle might like to act out. There are lots of books in the library on fairy tales. Get together and choose one. If you like, you can make your own original changes to the story."

Mary had already made herself the boss of our group. She corralled Song

Lee, Ida, ZuZu, Sid, Harry, and me at the table by the window. Everyone sat down except Harry. He was looking outside. It was just starting to rain.

"We need to pick a simple fairy tale," Mary declared. "It's easier to make a skit if the tale isn't too complicated. That's what the teacher said."

Harry turned around. "How about 'The Emperor's New Clothes'?" he suggested. "That tale is simple. The guy is naked as a jay and walks in a parade. I

could be the emperor and wear my long johns. All you'd have to do is clap for me as I walked by." Then Harry strutted around our library table like he was royalty. His nose was in the air.

Mary and Ida groaned.

"That is not happening, Harry Spooger!" Mary said firmly.

The rest of us giggled.

"How about 'The Musicians of Bremen'?" ZuZu said. "There are neat parts for a donkey, dog, cat, and rooster."

"Is there a bug in it?" Harry asked.

"*No!*" Mary scolded. "That tale is way too violent. All the animals kick and pinch and scratch the robbers."

"But that's how they get rid of them," ZuZu replied. "It's a happy ending."

"No," Mary snapped. "We're not fighting!"

"How about 'Goldilocks and the Three Bears'?" Sid suggested. "That's real easy."

"It sure is! We practically know the lines already!" Mary replied, twisting her braids.

"I can do the sets and costumes," Song Lee said. She didn't like speaking parts.

"Can I help?" Harry said. If there is one thing that Harry loves more than horrible things, it's Song Lee. I remember when he first noticed her in kindergarten. Song Lee brought a potato beetle for show-and-tell. Harry took one look at the beetle and one look at Song Lee. It has been true love ever since.

"Sure," Song Lee answered with a big smile. "Want to sketch the inside of the bears' house, Harry?" She took out some paper and Magic Markers. Harry squeezed next to her and shared her chair.

"I'll make earwigs on the bears' mop," he said.

Mary rolled her eyes but didn't complain. Harry was sitting down and working on something.

"I'm into earwigs right now, Mare," Harry explained. "I found a whole mess of them in my basement. They actually were on an old mop. And"—Harry held up one finger—"I found one in the dirt today." Harry pulled out a Kleenex from his pocket and unwrapped it. "I don't think he lived too long."

Edward, I thought.

Mary and Ida started to scream but immediately covered their mouths.

Miss Mackle didn't hear their muffled sounds. She was playing something on the computer with a few kids at the other end of the library. It sounded like an animated fairy tale.

Sid jumped out of his chair and got permission to go to the bathroom.

Song Lee made prayer hands.

"You'll be able to draw a real earwig now," ZuZu said calmly. "You can observe his head, abdomen, and thorax."

"He is . . . dead, right?" Mary asked.

"Dead as a doornail," Harry said. Then he started sketching Edward.

"I guess we could add one earwig," Mary said. "Miss Mackle said we could make changes."

"The bears do live in the woods," Song Lee added, "so there probably are bugs in their cabin."

"I better make three earwigs," Harry said. "The bugs should be in groups of three or seven. Those are important numbers in fairy tales. Sid told me."

Mary raised her eyebrows. She was impressed. "Okay, we have our fairy tale. We have our stage managers for scenery and costumes! Now we just need to decide who is who in the play. We need a cast."

When Sidney returned from the

bathroom, he sat at the opposite end of the table from Song Lee and Harry. He got his sock cap out of his jeans' back pocket and pulled it down over his ears.

"I'll be a bear!" ZuZu said.

"Me too," Sid and I joined in.

"Good, and I'll be Goldilocks!" Mary exclaimed.

"But I want to be Goldilocks," Ida replied.

"I said it first," Mary insisted.

"That's not fair," Ida replied. "We should pick straws or something."

Harry and Song Lee kept drawing while Ida and Mary argued. The rest of us talked about bears.

"I'm not gonna be Baby Bear," Sid said. "No way!"

"I'll be Baby Bear," ZuZu said. "I don't mind. He has the best lines."

"I'm Papa Bear," I said quickly.

Suddenly Sid's eyes bugged out. He knew what bear part was left.

"Oh, man!" Sid groaned. "I have to be Mama Bear?"

"Yup," ZuZu said. "We each got one choice."

"You'll be a great mama," Harry said with a wink.

Sid pulled his sock cap over his eyes as he sank into his chair.

Bugs and the Royal Dessert

At lunchtime, our class walked down to the cafeteria. Song Lee and Harry were still talking about the play. I was at the end of the line. When we got inside, everyone looked around and gasped.

"Look!" Sid shouted. "There are stars on the ceiling!"

Mary pointed to the neon sign over the door. It said STARLIGHT CAFÉ.

"What's going on?" Harry blurted out.

Mrs. Funderburke greeted everyone. "Welcome to the Starlight Café! Do you like it?"

All of us cheered.

"I thought our cafeteria needed a new look," the head cook chuckled. "Our custodian, Mr. Beausoleil, helped me put up the sparkly stars and plug in the sign that was donated by the Starlight Café in town. They're getting a bigger neon sign."

"How cool is that!" Harry blurted out.

"And," Miss Funderburke continued, "you may notice we also have a round table."

There it was in the corner by the drinking fountain. It had a red tablecloth, a vase of flowers, linen napkins, real glasses, and shiny silverware!

"It's suitable for kings and queens!"

Mrs. Funderburke said. "I thought it was time to bring a little royalty to the cafeteria. Especially now since the entire third grade is reading fairy tales."

"Right!" Sid said. "My stepdad and I've been reading fairy tales every night. Lots of them have kings and queens in them."

Mrs. Funderburke smiled as she held up two fingers. "Each day I will pick two names from each classroom. Those people will eat at the round table and practice good manners. They will also get a royal dessert."

Mrs. Funderburke stepped over to a card table with three glass jars. Then she reached into the first one, which said Room 3A. We all watched her unroll two small pieces of paper and read the names. They were both girls. Immediately they began jumping up and down. The second jar was our classroom's. "Now I will reach into Room 3B's jar."

She pulled out two pieces of paper and read the first name.

"Mary Berg."

Mary giggled and clapped her hands. "It's me! Lucky me! I'm going to be at a queen's table! This is going to be my favorite lunch ever!"

All the girls crossed their fingers. They wanted to be picked next. The boys in Room 3B inched back. I know I didn't want to sit at the Round Table. Not with three girls!

"Harry Spooger!" Mrs. Funderburke called out.

I tried not to laugh, but it was a little funny. Harry didn't smile or say a word.

A couple of the guys covered their mouths so no one would hear their snickers.

When Mrs. Funderburke drew the last two names from Room 3C, she chuckled. "I can't believe it! Two more girls! Well, Harry, this is your lucky day. You get to eat at the Round Table in the Starlight Café with five third-grade girls."

Harry turned and looked at the boys. "Anybody laughs, and they'll find an earwig in their ear!"

Nobody moved except Sidney. He put his hands over his ears!

After Harry left, most of us went through the cafeteria line to get a tray

of spaghetti and meatballs. I sat next to Dexter and ZuZu. Sidney sat across from me.

"The stars on the ceiling are cool," Dexter said. "I wonder how many there are."

"Eighty-eight," ZuZu replied. "I just counted them."

Dexter slurped a noodle. "Look at Harry," he said. "He's wearing a crown just like the girls! Now he's putting a linen napkin on his lap. I bet he's miserable."

"What do you think the royal dessert is?" Sid asked.

"I'm going to find out," I said. I really wanted to check on Harry. I was a little worried about him. Harry is my best friend even if he forgets me sometimes. I raised my hand for the lunch aide.

"May I get a drink of water, please?" I asked.

After I got permission, I took a long drink at the fountain and listened.

Harry was talking about earwigs.

"Actually," he said, "they can dig six feet underground."

"Puh-leese," Mary said. "We're eating, Harry."

Harry flashed his white teeth. "So do earwigs. It's fascinating, really. They use their long pincers to grab aphids or dead bugs or plants or rotten vegetables." When he popped a meatball in his mouth, Mary made a face. So did another girl.

Two of the third-grade girls were interested, though. "I wonder what they look like," one said.

"I'll show you," Harry said as he reached into his pocket.

Oh, no! I thought. He was getting Edward!

I rushed over to the Royal Table. "How's it going?" I boldly interrupted.

"Hey, Doug-o!" Harry replied.

"Eh . . . how's the royal dessert?" I asked, hoping to change the subject.

"Great!" Mary said. "It's petit fours. That's French for small frosted cakes. They're delicious! Quite a delicacy."

"I'm going to eat three," Harry said. His hand was still in his pocket. "Now, how many of you want to see what an earwig looks like?"

Four girls raised their hands. Mary was the only one who didn't. She closed her eyes tight.

I took a step back. The girls' reaction was going to be deadly and *loud*!

Slowly Harry pulled something out of his pocket.

He unrolled a piece of paper, then held it up.

"What a great earwig!" a girl said.

"You draw insects so well!" another said.

"Thanks," Harry replied. "I labeled

the head, thorax, and abdomen. This is a male earwig because their pincers are more bow-legged."

"It looks so real!" a third girl said.

Mary let out a long sigh. I knew she was thankful it wasn't the real bug.

I strolled back to my lunch table. Harry was doing just fine. I wasn't so sure about Mary, though. I don't think that was her favorite lunch! She really got bugged by Harry!

The Earwig Scare!

The next day Miss Mackle borrowed Sid's green book and read us "Little Red Riding Hood."

"I thought it was neat how the wolf talked," Ida said.

"Lots of times animals and objects talk in fairy tales," Sid replied.

"Was there a lesson to be learned in the story?" the teacher asked.

Mary immediately raised her hand. "Yes! Do not talk to strangers!"

"Good," the teacher replied. "I hope everyone remembers that important rule! Now, you may meet with your literature circles and talk about your skits."

Our group met on the moon rug in the library corner of Room 3B. "So, who can come to my house Saturday at one o'clock?" Sid asked.

All of us raised our hands. "Mom said it was fine," Ida replied.

"Me too," ZuZu said.

"My grandma said I could bring snacks for everyone," Harry added. "And my beanbag chair for a prop."

"I have three bear costumes," Song Lee added. "Mom got them at a party store for seventy-five percent off because it isn't Halloween. Harry and I are still painting the mural."

"I finished drawing my three ear-wigs," Harry said. "I cut them out, and Grandma is laminating them for me."

"Maybe we should add them to our story," ZuZu said. "It could be funny, like those fractured fairy tales are."

Harry clicked his fingers. "ZuZu! You just gave me a whopper of an idea. I'm going to write a few changes for our play!"

Song Lee clapped her hands. "Good!" she beamed. "It will be fun!"

I noticed Mary and Ida had been quiet the whole time.

"So who's Goldilocks?" I asked.

Ida folded her arms. "Mary doesn't want to pick straws."

"Okay, guys," Harry said, "it's a no-brainer. We have to have a Goldilocks.

So, I'm cooking up an idea how to choose one. It will be fair and square."

Mary groaned. "How can we be sure it's one hundred percent fair, Harry Spooger?"

"Because I'm getting my grandma to help!"

"Huh?" Mary and Ida replied.

"You'll see," Harry replied. "At Sid's house."

Saturday, my mom walked me over to Sidney's house. He lived on the same block as Song Lee.

As we passed her house, I could see Harry and Song Lee sitting on the lowest limb of a maple tree. There was a long plastic rope dangling from the top limb. They were shaking it and laughing.

"Hi, Harry!" my mom called.

I just waved.

They both waved back. "Hi!" Song Lee said. "We found lots of earwigs!"

"They're falling from the tree!" Harry said. "Want to see?"

"No thanks," I called back. "I'll see you at Sid's."

"See you! We'll be leaving in a jiff!" Harry said.

Mom and I continued walking.

"Is something bothering you?" Mom asked.

"Nope," I said.

"Are you sure?"

"Yup," I said.

"Well, I think it's nice you and Harry play with different people," Mom said.

"Yeah," I groaned. "I don't really like bugs."

"You don't have to," Mom replied. "Friends can have different interests."

When we knocked on Sid's door, his stepdad answered. He was wearing a sweatshirt that said GEORGE LaFLEUR'S TOMBSTONES. "Hi, Doug, come on in. The kids are in the kitchen waiting for you."

"Cool," I said. "Bye, Mom."

When I walked in, Sid and ZuZu were walking around like bears. Sid was hunched over a little. ZuZu was squatting as he walked. Mary and Ida rushed over to me.

"Where's Harry and Song Lee?" they asked.

"They're coming. They were up in a tree shaking down earwigs," I said.

Sidney immediately ran out of the

room. When he returned, he had on yellow earmuffs.

"What are you doing?" Mary asked.

"Protecting my ears," Sid said. "Why do you think those bugs are called earwigs? *They like ears!*"

We all took a step back.

"You know Harry," Sid continued. "He's going to bring an earwig with him." Then he lowered his voice. "Do you know what earwigs do?"

"Crawl into your ears?" ZuZu asked.

"Yup!" Sid snapped. "*Then* they burrow into your brains and lay eggs. The next thing you know, those buggers hatch. Bingo! You have baby earwigs crawling out of your nose and eyeballs."

"*Aaaaaauuuuugh!*" we all screamed.

When the doorbell rang, we all ran into the living room to hide from Harry!

Mr. LaFleur answered the door. I could hear him say, "Come on in! The kids are in the kitchen. They're having a noisy rehearsal!"

I was hiding behind the big TV. No one could see me, but after I got down on my knees, I could peek around the TV stand. I could see Harry and Song Lee in the kitchen.

"The kids were just here a minute ago," Mr. LaFleur said.

Harry started taking out plastic flowerpots from his sack. "After I pass these snacks out, I'll go look for them."

"Unusual snacks," Mr. LaFleur said.

"It's Grandma's recipe, but I helped. I love making Dirt Pudding."

Song Lee laid her rolled-up mural and costumes in a pile on the floor. Then she walked into the living room. "Mary? Ida?" she called.

Harry walked into the living room too. "Doug? ZuZu? Sid?"

No one answered.

"They must be hiding," Mr. LaFleur said. "Guess we'll have to start looking for them."

Harry looked under the coffee table. "Not here!"

Song Lee looked behind the curtains. "Not here!"

Harry leaned over the couch. "Howdy, howdy!" he said.

Sid and ZuZu slowly came out.

When Song Lee peeked around the TV, she spotted me.

"Doug!"

I came out slowly too.

Just as Harry opened the closet, the girls screamed. "Aha! I found you!" he said.

"Okay, everyone, time-out!" Mr. LaFleur said. "Let's have a chat on the living-room rug here."

We all sat down in a circle. Sid sat next to his stepdad.

"Am I sensing some fear here?" Mr. LaFleur said.

Sid started to inch behind his stepdad. "Does H-H-Harry have any earwigs?"

"Just Edward," he said.

"Who's Edward?" everyone said.

"A dead earwig," I replied.

Harry pulled a Kleenex out of his pocket and gently unfolded it. "I want to give him a burial."

We all stared at Edward.

Then Mr. LaFleur looked at Harry. "You like earwigs?"

"I love all kinds of bugs," Harry replied, "but Edward is extraordinary. He helped me draw pictures for our play."

"Well Sid, here, has a fear of them. Can you help him out?" Mr. LaFleur asked.

"What are you afraid of?" Harry asked. "The liquid they squirt? It is smelly. But earwigs can't hurt you."

"I didn't know they could squirt stuff," Sid said, adjusting his earmuffs. "I know they like to go inside people's ears. That's why they call them earwigs. *And that's why I'm wearing earmuffs!*"

Harry refolded the tissue over

Edward and set him down gently on the end table. "I got a book on earwigs out of the library," Harry said. "Long, long ago, people thought earwigs could crawl in your ears and bore a hole in your brain. But that's not true."

"I didn't think so," ZuZu said. "But I wasn't sure."

"So it's a myth," Mr. LaFleur said. "It's untrue."

"Yup!" Harry replied.

"You mean earwigs don't like people's ears?" Sid said.

"Nope," Harry answered. "They like damp places, compost piles, trees after a rain, trash, places under boards, woodpiles, and basements."

Sid took off his earmuffs. "Free at last!" he exclaimed. "I even had a nightmare last night about earwigs. Now I

can just laugh at it!" He ran over and
gave Harry a hug!

Harry fell over backwards.

When he sat back up, he asked Mr.
LaFleur a question. "Do you have a
garden?"

"I do, Harry, but I haven't planted
anything yet. It's too early."

"Could I bury Edward in it?"

"Sure can," Mr. LaFleur answered.

Then Harry popped another big
question.

The Goldilocks
Worm-Off

"Who wants to help me bury Edward?" Harry asked.

We all raised our hands. Even Sidney.

We followed Harry out to the backyard. He dug a hole in one corner of the garden. He placed the tissue with Edward in it inside the hole. We watched him sprinkle dirt on top until he made a mound. Harry then patted it with the palm of his hand. Song Lee found three little rocks and placed them on top. Mary added some blades of grass. Ida added a few sticks.

"We should say a prayer," I said.

"Yeah," Harry agreed. "Will you say one, Song Lee?"

Song Lee nodded, then spoke very softly. "Dear God, help us love every living thing."

"Amen," we all said.

When we came back into the kitchen, we washed our hands and stared at

Harry's snack. Each pot had a name on it, except for two.

Mary and Ida's names were missing.

"Which one is mine?" Mary asked.

"Yeah," Ida added. "There's no name on these two."

Harry flashed his white teeth. "Those two pots are for our Goldilocks Worm-Off!"

"Huh?" we all said.

"I've heard of bake-offs," Mary said, "but not worm-offs!"

Harry explained. "Everyone sit down except for you and Ida."

We did. I sat down by the pot that said DOUG. Everyone else found their name on their pot and sat down too.

"Grandma and I made this special snack," Harry said. "It's the fairest way I know for choosing Goldilocks."

"We're eating what's inside this pot?" Sid said.

"Yup!" Harry replied.

"Eeyew, it looks like dirt!" Mary said, still standing up.

"It is," Harry replied. "It's dirt pudding."

"Oh, Harry!" Mary exclaimed. "That's a horrible snack."

"No, it isn't," I said. "I've had it at Harry's house before. It's really delicious. You'll see."

"Now, Ida and Mary, you pick one of the two pots that has no name." Harry pointed them out. They were right next to each other.

Mary and Ida walked back and forth. They couldn't decide which pot to choose.

Watching them was like watching a

ball in a tennis game. Back and forth, back and forth. Finally, Mary plopped down in a seat and Ida took the seat next to her.

"Now what?" Mary said.

"Start eating. Whoever finds a worm inside their pudding gets to be Goldilocks."

"A worm?" everyone replied.

"They're gummy worms," I said. "Candy."

Everyone sighed with relief.

We all started tasting the dirt pudding.

"Mmmm," Ida said. "It's creamy chocolate."

"Are these crushed Oreos on top?" ZuZu asked.

"Yup," Harry said. "I crushed them with a hammer."

"The same hammer you use on rusty nails?" Mary asked. We all stopped eating.

"Yup, but Grandma tied a baggy on the end."

Phew! I thought.

No one said anything more. We just kept our eyes on Mary and Ida. And as we ate our pudding, we all wondered: Who was going to find the gummy worm?

"Well, it is fair," Ida said as she licked her lips.

"It is," Mary agreed. "And I think the person who isn't Goldilocks should be the narrator."

"That's a good idea!" Ida replied.

Halfway through the dirt pudding, most of us found our gummy worms. "Are you sure you put one in mine?" Ida asked.

"I put one in yours or Mary's way down in the bottom," Harry said with a grin. "Keep eating."

Mary half laughed. "I never thought I would hope to find a slimy horrible thing in my pudding. But I sure do now!"

Three minutes later, one of them called out, *"I found a worm!"*

It was Ida! She was holding it between two fingers.

You couldn't see what color the gummy worm was, because it was coated in chocolate pudding.

Mary's eyes got a little watery, but she was a good sport. "Okay," she said, "Ida is Goldilocks. I'm the narrator. I get to tell the story."

"Cool!" Harry said. "Now I want to tell you about the changes I made to our play. Instead of calling it 'Goldilocks and the Three Bears,' I thought we could call it 'Goldilocks and the Three Bugs.'"

All of us laughed, even Mary.

Harry took out a pad of paper. He had written four long pages. "This play is dedicated to Edward the Earwig," he said.

We listened as he read each page.

Sid laughed so hard he fell off his chair.

"I like it!" ZuZu said.

"I love it!" Song Lee added.

Mary and Ida clapped. Then Mary added, "I have to add some lines for the narrator, of course."

"Sure!" Harry replied.

"Let's do it!" I said.

After we practiced the skit for an hour, we felt good about things. I just wondered if Miss Mackle and the rest of the class would like our play. It was time for Harry to bug the whole class!

"Goldilocks and the Three Bugs"

Monday morning was a special day. We moved our desks back to make room for a stage. Everyone sat on the floor.

When it was our turn, Mary introduced our skit. "My group made changes to the classic folk story 'Goldilocks and the Three Bears.' We now call it, 'Goldilocks and the Three Bugs.'"

The children giggled. Miss Mackle laughed.

"Our playwright is Harry Spooger;

however, I wrote the narrator's part."

When everyone clapped, Harry and Mary took a deep bow.

Song Lee and Harry quickly taped their mural on the blackboard. It was a picture of the inside of the bears' log cabin.

Song Lee had drawn family pictures on the wall, a pot of porridge cooking in the fireplace, and vases on the windowsill. Harry had added the earwigs, spiders, and stinkbugs.

"How come there are so many bugs in the cabin?" Dexter asked.

"Because the bears live in the middle of the woods," Mary explained.

"Cool. I like stinkbugs," Dexter added.

Harry turned around and flashed a toothy smile.

Mary beamed. "We hope you enjoy 'Goldilocks and the Three Bugs.'"

Then she moved to the left of the stage and began reading her narrator's part. "Once upon a time there were three bears who lived in a cabin in the woods. Papa Bear, Mama Bear, and Baby Bear. Every morning, they took a walk while their porridge cooled. Today, while they were in the woods, a little girl stopped by their cabin."

Ida skipped onstage. She was wearing a wig, a pretty dress, and a red ribbon.

"Oh, what a cute little cabin!" Ida exclaimed. "Hmmm . . . No one's home. I think I'll go inside." As Ida looked around, she noticed three bowls of porridge on the kitchen table.

"I will try this bowl of porridge first," Ida said. "Oh! It is too hot!"

I liked the way Ida waved her hand in front of her mouth.

"Now I will try the next bowl. Man! This is too cold!" Ida said, making her whole body shiver.

We watched Ida try the third bowl of porridge. After she took a small spoonful she smiled at the audience. "This porridge is just right!"

Mary continued the story. "Goldilocks scooped up some more of the scrumptious porridge, then stared at something crawling on her spoon."

"Aaauuugh!" Ida yelled. *"It's a bug!"*

Ida held it up so the audience could see. It was a big, laminated earwig that Harry had drawn.

Everyone groaned, *"Eeyew!"*

Ida dropped the bug on the floor. "Yuck!" she said. Then she froze in place until the stage managers were ready.

Song Lee rushed a small chair to the stage. It was borrowed from the kindergarten room. Harry scooted in one of the chairs from Room 3B and added a pillow. Then both Harry and Song Lee brought Miss Mackle's chair to the front of the room.

Ida stopped standing like a statue. She walked over to the big chair and sat down.

"Ouch!" she yelled. "This chair is too hard. My buns hurt!"

Lots of kids giggled.

Ida tried the chair with the pillow next. "Ohhhhhh! This is too soft and mushy."

Ida walked over to the kindergarten chair. Just as she was about to sit down, she screamed. *"AAAAAaaaaugh! There's a bug on this chair!"*

Ida held up the second bug!

The audience roared when they saw the big earwig.

Mary cleared her throat. It was time for her to read again. "Goldilocks was so tired, she decided to go upstairs and look for a bed to take a nap on."

Ida yawned as she marched in place for about a minute. While she was stepping in place, Song Lee and Harry got the props ready: a pillow, a blanket, and a beanbag chair.

Ida stretched her arms out. "I'm pooped," she said. "I'll try one of these three beds." She lay down on the beanbag chair first. "Oh, this is too soft and mushy."

Ida tried the blanket next. "Oh, man!" she said. "This bed is too hard."

Ida tested out the third bed. It was the pillow. "This is warm and cozy," she said. "Just right!" As soon as Ida closed her eyes, Harry tiptoed up behind her and taped something on her forehead.

"Poor Goldilocks!" Mary read from her script. "She slept soundly, and had no idea there was a critter on her forehead. Goldilocks also had no idea that the three bears had returned from the woods, and were entering the cabin right now!"

"Time to go, Doug!" ZuZu whispered to me.

I started walking onstage like Papa Bear. It sure was warm inside my costume. Sid and I were hunched over. ZuZu squatted to look like Baby Bear. I spoke first in a deep voice.

"I'm Papa Bear. The boss. It's time to get some grub!"

"I hope you like the porridge I made, dear," Sid said in a high voice. "I made it special."

Everyone laughed when Sidney talked like a girl.

"Tum-tum wants a yum-yum," ZuZu said in a baby voice.

Now kids were giggling.

We pretended to gobble down the porridge.

"That was deeeeelicious," I said. "Did you add something extra, Mama Bear?"

"Yes I did, Papa Bear," Sid said, in a high voice again. "I added a few bugs for flavor!"

"Mmmmm, buggy-wuggy," ZuZu said.

All three of us got up from the table and marched in place.

Mary continued her reading. "The bears lumbered upstairs for a nap. When they got to their bedroom, they were in for a surprise."

"Someone's been sleeping in my bed!" I said in a deep voice.

"Someone's been sleeping in *my* bed!" Sid said in a high voice.

ZuZu leaned over and looked at Ida in his bed. "Buggy-wuggy!" he said.

The three of us stood over Ida and stared at the earwig on her forehead.

Ida suddenly sat up.

"Buggy-wuggy!" ZuZu repeated.

"Where?" Ida asked.

"There!" we all said, pointing to her forehead.

Ida pulled the earwig off and looked at it. "*Aaaaauuuugh!*" she screamed. "I'm out of here!" Ida handed the bug to Mama Bear, then jumped off the pillow, marched in place, and ran offstage.

Then Mary read Harry's ending. "The bears were so sleepy they didn't bother chasing Goldilocks out the door. The bug did that job for them."

"I think we should keep this earwig for a pet," I said.

Sid nodded. "I think so too, dear. But we should give him a name."

"Buggy-wuggy?" ZuZu said.

"No," I replied. "We'll call him Edward."

Mary said the last words of the play. "The earwig had saved the bears from their intruder! He deserved a long life. The end."

Everyone sitting on the floor clapped and cheered.

Mary put down her script and said, "Now I would like to introduce each of the characters, and our stage managers."

She had us each take a final bow.

After everyone clapped again, Miss Mackle stood up. "Your fractured fairy tale was so much fun! What a surprise ending! Do you think your play had a

lesson to be learned?" she asked.

"It sure did," Harry answered. "If you break into someone's house, beware! You could be bugged!"

"Bravo!" Miss Mackle said.

At lunch recess, a group of us ran outside to the kickball diamond. Harry had the ball and ran to the pitcher's mound. I played fielding pitcher right next to him.

At last, I thought. No more bugs. How cool is that!

"Okay, you guys," Harry yelled to the kids who were lining up at the plate to kick. "What's the name of your team?"

"We're the Mighty Yankees!" Dexter replied. "Who are you?"

"The Earwigs," Harry replied with a smile.

I rolled my eyes.

"The *Extraordinary* Earwigs," Mary added from first base.

I shook my head.

I never thought my story could end with bugs and still be happy, but it is. Sometimes when Harry bugs you, it can be a lot of fun.

"Go Extraordinary Earwigs," Song Lee called from shortstop.

"Play ball!" I yelled.

"Goldilocks and the Three Bugs"

(Dedicated to Edward the Earwig)

Characters:

Narrator   Mama Bear

Goldilocks   Baby Bear

Papa Bear

Props:

golden wig   3 earwig cutouts

3 bowls   3 spoons

blanket   bear costumes

pillow   small table

beanbag chair   3 different-sized chairs

mural of the inside of the bears' cabin

Setting:

A cabin in the woods

Time:

Morning

Narrator: Once upon a time there were three bears who lived in a cabin in the woods: Papa Bear, Mama Bear, and Baby Bear. Every morning, they took a walk while their porridge cooled. Today while they were in the woods, a little girl stopped by their cabin.

Goldilocks: Oh, what a cute little cabin! Hmm . . . No one's home. I think I'll go inside.

Narrator: As Goldilocks looked around, she noticed three bowls of porridge on the kitchen table.

Goldilocks: I will try this bowl of porridge first. Oh! It is too hot! Now I will try the next bowl. Man! This is too cold!

Narrator: When Goldilocks tried the third bowl of porridge, she smiled.

Goldilocks: This porridge is just right!

Narrator: Goldilocks scooped up some more of the scrumptious porridge, then stared at something crawling on her spoon.

Goldilocks: *Aaauugh! It's a bug! Yuck!*

Narrator: Goldilocks dropped the bug on the kitchen floor. Then, she went into the living room and sat in the big chair.

Goldilocks: Ouch! This chair is too hard. My buns hurt!

Goldilocks: Ohhhhhh! This is too soft and mushy!

Goldilocks: *Aaaaauuuugh! There's a bug on this chair!*

Narrator: Goldilocks was so tired she decided to go upstairs and look for a bed to take a nap on.

Goldilocks: (*Yawns as she walks in place*) I'm pooped! I'll try one of these three beds. Oh, this is too soft and mushy! Oh, man! This bed is too hard!

Goldilocks: This is warm and cozy. Just right!

(*Stage manager tapes one earwig to her forehead.*)

Narrator: Poor Goldilocks! She slept soundly and

had no idea there was a critter on her forehead. Goldilocks also had no idea that the three bears had returned from the woods and were entering the cabin right now!

Papa Bear: I'm Papa Bear. The boss. It's time to get some grub!

Mama Bear: I hope you like the porridge I made, dear. I made it special.

Baby Bear: Tum-tum wants a yum-yum!

Narrator: The three bears gobbled down their porridge.

Papa Bear: That was deeeelicious! Did you add something extra, Mama Bear?

Mama Bear: Yes, I did, Papa Bear. I added a few bugs for flavor!

Baby Bear: Mmmmm . . . buggy-wuggy!

Narrator: The bears lumbered upstairs for a nap. When they got to their bedroom, they were in for a surprise.

Papa Bear: Someone's been sleeping in my bed!

Mama Bear: Someone's been sleeping in *my* bed!

Baby Bear: Buggy-wuggy! Buggy-wuggy!

Goldilocks: Where?

All three bears together: There!

Goldilocks: *Aaauuuggh!* I'm out of here.

Narrator: The bears were so sleepy they didn't bother chasing Goldilocks out the door. The bug did that job for them.

Papa Bear: I think we should keep this earwig for a pet.

Mama Bear: I think so too, dear. But we should give him a name.

Baby Bear: Buggy-wuggy?

Papa Bear: No, we'll call him Edward.

Narrator: The earwig had saved the bears from their intruder! He deserved a long life. The end.